P9-DBM-988

To our animal friends everywhere. We love you.

GROSSET & DUNLAP
Published by the Penguin Group
Penguin Group (USA) Inc., 375 Hudson Street, New York, New York 10014, USA

USA | Canada | UK | Ireland | Australia | New Zealand | India | South Africa | China
Penguin Books Ltd, Registered Offices: 80 Strand, London WC2R 0RL, England

For more information about the Penguin Group visit penguin.com

All rights reserved. No part of this book may be reproduced, scanned, or distributed in any printed or electronic form without permission. Please do not participate in or encourage piracy of copyrighted materials in violation of the author's rights. Purchase only authorized editions.

Text copyright © 2009 by Sue Bentley. Illustrations copyright © 2009 by Angela Swan. Cover illustration © 2009 by Andrew Farley. First printed in Great Britain in 2009 by Penguin Books Ltd. First published in the United States in 2013 by Grosset & Dunlap, a division of Penguin Young Readers Group, 345 Hudson Street, New York, New York 10014. GROSSET & DUNLAP is a trademark of Penguin Group (USA) Inc. Printed in the U.S.A.

Library of Congress Cataloging-in-Publication Data is available.

ISBN 978-0-448-46736-8 10 9 8 7 6 5 4 3 2 1

ALWAYS LEARNING PEARSON

A Christmas Wish

A Christmas Wish

SUE BENTLEY

illustrated by Angela Swan

Grosset & Dunlap
An Imprint of Penguin Group (USA) Inc.

Prologue

"I'm coming, too!" Starshine cried, galloping toward the ice bridge after the White Crystal Reindeer Herd. As he lifted his head, his chocolate-brown eyes flashed with determination.

It would be a long journey through the night sky to deliver presents to children all over the world. But Starshine had been practicing by leaping high over the snow-covered trees and galloping among the stars. He knew he was ready to join the other reindeer.

Moonlight gleamed on the young reindeer's fluffy white coat and glowing gold antlers and hooves. The tiny gold snow globe he wore on a chain around his neck tinkled softly.

"Yay!" Starshine cried, and, with a twitch of his short tail, he soared up into the night sky.

Just ahead of him galloped his older brothers, Moonfleet and Dazzler. The herd stretched into a single line as they sped ever higher, leaving a silvery trail of hoofprints behind them in the air.

Starshine panted a little as he strained to keep up.

Suddenly there was a bright flash

and an enormous reindeer with a wise expression appeared next to him. He had a thick golden neck ruff and magnificent spreading antlers.

"Father!"

Starshine puffed out his little chest. How proud of him the reindeer king must be.

"I know that you are eager to run with us, Starshine. But you are not yet ready for this task. Turn back now," the king said gently in a deep, soft voice.

"But I am strong and fast!" Starshine protested. "Please let me go with you!"

The king shook his head, his deep amber eyes gleaming with affection. "That is not possible, my son. We have a long way to go and many presents to deliver. I am afraid that you would hold us up."

"I won't," Starshine began. "I promise—"

"That is enough," the king said firmly. "Return to Ice Mountain Castle, Starshine. We will speak of this later."

The young reindeer bowed his head. "Yes, Father." He hung back a little as his father rejoined the herd. They disappeared into the night and their trail of shimmering silver hoofprints began to grow fainter.

Starshine glanced dejectedly over his shoulder. His icy home world was just visible far below him. Why did *he* have to return to their castle just because he was the youngest? It wasn't fair. Moonfleet and Dazzler had all the fun.

He'd prove to them all that he *could* keep up! On impulse, the young magic reindeer leaped forward again. His breath came fast as he galloped through the star-pricked blackness.

But where was the trail? He couldn't see a single glowing hoofprint. Starshine kicked at the air in panic; his legs felt so heavy.

"Help! I'm lost!" he bleated. But there was no one to hear him. The golden snow globe around his neck began to glow. There was a flash of dazzling bright light, and a starry mist of silver and gold surrounded him. Starshine snorted weakly as he felt the magic envelop him and float him gently downward . . .

Chapter ONE

"Marie Zaleski?" the class teacher called, looking up from the attendance book.

"Yes, sir!" Marie answered. She blushed as there was a ripple of laughter from the girls sitting at the desk opposite.

"You're supposed to say, 'Here, Mr. Carpenter,'" Shannon James said. "But he wouldn't understand you anyway!"

Shannon was the most popular girl in the class. She had shiny dark-brown hair and a pretty, heart-shaped face.

Marie went even redder. She had lived in Poland for most of her nine years. She spoke perfect English, but Shannon took every opportunity to tease her about her accent.

"I like the way Marie talks. It's different," said a boy's voice from the desk next to Shannon. It was Chris Robins, a lively boy with a playful expression who was always joking around.

Marie turned and darted a quick, shy look at him.

"Yeah, right!" Shannon crowed, grinning. "You would say that, Chris!"

There was another burst of laughter. As Chris joined in, Marie sank down in her seat. Maybe he'd only been pretending to stick up for her, so he could tease her even more. She shook her head slowly as she thought that she didn't understand these kids. They often said one thing and meant another.

"All right, class. Quiet down," Mr. Carpenter ordered, closing the attendance book. "Open your history textbooks, please. We'll continue reading about how the Victorians celebrated Christmas. After morning break, we'll start making classroom decorations."

"Mr. Carpenter?" Shannon put up her hand. "Is it true that this year's play is going to be a musical?"

"That's right. We'll be choosing people to play the lead roles tomorrow or the day after," the teacher explained.

"Great!" Shannon wiggled excitedly. "I'm going to be Mary, Baby Jesus's mother!" she said confidently.

Mr. Carpenter smiled. "Are you sure? That's a big part with some difficult songs."

"Shannon's got a really good voice!" Chris called out. "You just wait until you hear it!"

Shannon grinned smugly as there was a cheer from her classmates. Marie didn't know whether she should join in. She decided not to, in case she drew more attention to herself, and bent over her textbook instead.

On one page there was a picture of a Victorian family standing around a prettily decorated Christmas tree with colorful wrapped presents at its base. Outside the window, carolers stood in the snow. It looked like the perfect family Christmas. Marie sighed unhappily, wishing that *her* family could all be together for this first Christmas in America. But her dad had stayed behind in Poland because his sister was sick. Marie and her mom were staying with Gran and Gramps, and Dad was hoping to join them soon.

Marie glanced out of a nearby window where the playground was just visible through lashing rain. Everything was gray, damp, and miserable. The morning seemed to drag on forever. But she cheered up a little after the break when they started on the decorations.

Marie loved making things, and she was really good at it. After folding up some white paper, she carefully cut out shapes along the fold lines. When she opened the paper it turned into a pretty garland of lacy snowflakes.

As she dabbed on glue and sprinkled on dustings of silver glitter, she thought of Poland. It had been snowing when she and her family left. Everything was gleaming white. The air was crisp and so cold it made your nose prickle to breathe. *This snowflake garland reminds me of home*, she thought.

And then she remembered, with a pang, that *this* was now her home.

Deep in thought, she didn't notice Chris creeping up behind her with a rubber-band stretched across his fingers like a catapult.

"Hey! Marie!" he called. "That's a really cool decoration!"

Taken by surprise, she whipped around, just as he twanged the band at her. It pinged her forehead, just above her eyebrow.

"Ow!" she cried and, to her horror, felt tears stinging her eyes—even though it didn't actually hurt that much.

"Good shot, Chris!" Shannon crowed.

But Chris's face fell. "Sorry. It was a joke. I didn't mean—"

Marie didn't want to hear it. She'd had enough of these mean, unfriendly kids.

"Yes you did!" she cried, her temper rising. "Why don't you just leave me alone?" Jumping to her feet, she ran toward the door. "I . . . I need to go to the bathroom," she murmured to the surprised teacher as she hurtled past him.

She only meant to go and sit in the coatroom until she calmed down. But somehow her feet kept right on going, taking her outside and across the playground. She spotted the bleachers, which were out of sight of the classrooms, and dived behind them.

I hate it here! I wish we'd never come! she said to herself, wiping away tears with the back of her hand. It wasn't fair. Why couldn't her mom have found a new job in a children's hospital in Poland instead of here? Marie made a decision. She was going straight home to Gran and Gramps's house. And she was never coming back to this dumb school where everyone was too busy to bother with a new girl.

Maybe Mom will let me be homeschooled, she thought, as she prepared to make a dash for the school gate. She rocked forward on to her toes. *One! Two! Thr–*

Suddenly there was a bright flash of light, and a mist made up of millions of tiny gold and silver stars filled the air around her. Marie noticed glittery stars forming and twinkling on her skin.

"Oh!" She screwed up her eyes, trying to see through the strange shining mist.

As it cleared, Marie noticed a fluffy white reindeer with a softly glowing

coat and little golden antlers and hooves walking slowly toward her. Around its neck it wore something that looked like a tiny golden charm on a delicate chain.

It gave a scared little bleat. "Can you help me, please?"

Chapter TWO

Marie's eyes widened as she stared at the cute little reindeer in astonishment. She had no idea what it was doing here behind the school bleachers, but she was pretty sure that reindeer couldn't talk.

"Hello, there," she said softly, thinking she must be imagining it all. "Where did you come from?"

The reindeer's sensitive white ears

flickered, and she saw that it had big chocolate-brown eyes. "I have just arrived here. I was following my herd when I became lost. What is this place?"

Marie did a double take. She felt like pinching herself to make sure she wasn't

dreaming. But the little reindeer was looking intently at her, as if expecting an answer.

"This is . . . um, Chiltern Park Elementary School," she told him.

"I do not know this place. I think I am a long way from home," the reindeer said thoughtfully. "My name is Starshine of the White Crystal Herd. What is yours?"

"I—I'm Marie. Marie Zaleski," she stuttered, still not quite believing that she was actually talking to a reindeer. This was like something out of the Polish folktales her dad told her.

Starshine bent his knees and dipped his head in a formal bow. His golden antlers left a trail of sparkling bright light, which swiftly faded as he straightened up. "I am honored to meet you, Marie," he snorted softly.

"Um . . . likewise," Marie said, dipping her chin politely. "Where did you come from? And how come you can talk, if . . . um, you don't mind me asking," she added, keeping very still so that she wouldn't frighten this amazing creature away.

Starshine flicked his little moplike white tail. "All the White Crystal Reindeer can talk. We live in Ice Mountain Castle in a faraway world, with my father and mother, who are our king and queen. I have two older brothers, Dazzler and Moonfleet. I am the youngest reindeer in the herd"—Starshine lifted his head proudly—"but I am ready to do my duty and deliver presents all over the world to make people happy."

Marie was fascinated. She was still

trying to take this all in. The little reindeer's world sounded so strange and magical. Something he said puzzled her, though. "You deliver things all over the world? But how . . . ?"

"My magic snow globe helps me. I will show you," Starshine snuffled, backing away.

Marie felt a warm prickling sensation flowing down the back of her neck as what she had thought to be a tiny golden charm on the chain around his neck began to glow and get bigger. An image appeared inside the clear crystal globe.

Marie leaned forward curiously. She saw an amazing icy world of endless snow-covered peaks, blue glaciers, and frozen seas. Topping a massive cliff of ice was a tall building with spires and turrets.

It looked like a sparkling cathedral made of glass.

She saw Starshine—a tiny white shape standing on an icy platform. He glowed so brightly with golden light that Marie had to shade her eyes to look at him. Sparks glinted in his fur and his chocolate-brown eyes twinkled with gold. Around him were lots of older reindeer, all with sparkling white coats, large golden antlers, and golden hooves.

As she watched, a line of reindeer appeared in the sky above the castle, leaving a trail of sparkling golden hoofprints behind them. They swept downward and landed beside Starshine.

Marie realized that she was watching events that must have already happened before Starshine came to her world.

"Wow!" she breathed in total wonderment. She had never seen anything so beautiful in her entire life. Starshine was cute and pretty with his fluffy white coat and dewy eyes, but in his own world—surrounded by that dazzling halo of golden light—he was a magnificent sight. "Is that really where you live with the White Crystal Herd?"

Starshine nodded, his brown eyes now shadowed by homesickness. "Yes. That is Ice Mountain Castle," he told her with a little catch in his voice. "I followed the others when they left on a trip, but Father told me to go home. I thought I was strong enough to keep up. But I grew tired and became lost. My magic snow globe brought me here." Starshine dipped his head and looked up at her with big sad

eyes. "I miss my family very much. Will you help me find my way back to them?"

Marie's heart melted. She knew how it felt to be lonely and miss someone you loved who was far away. "Of course I'll help you. What do I have to do?"

Starshine flicked his little white ears and seemed to cheer up a bit. "We must watch the night sky together for a trail of sparkling hoofprints. It will be invisible to most people in this world, but you will be able to see it if you are with me or very close to me."

"All right. We'll keep a lookout for it," Marie said. "Maybe Mom and Gran and Gramps could help us, too? I can't wait to tell them about you!"

Starshine lifted his head. "I am sorry, Marie. You can tell no one about me or what I have told you."

Marie felt disappointed that she couldn't confide in anyone. But then she thought about how awful today had already been, and she decided that it might be nice to have a special secret of her own. She felt proud that Starshine had chosen her to help him. At least now she had a real friend who understood exactly how she felt.

"You must promise me, Marie," Starshine insisted, blinking at her with his intelligent eyes.

Marie nodded. She was determined to do all she could to keep Starshine safe and help him return to his magical ice world and his family. As she was wondering whether or not to leave for home now—and take Starshine with her—a girl walked behind the bleachers.

It was Shannon James.

"Mr. Carpenter sent me to find you. I've been looking everywhere for you. Why are you hiding out here?" she asked.

Marie panicked. Any minute now Shannon was going to see the little magic reindeer! Marie had to do something. Spreading her arms wide, she did a funny little sideways shuffle that hid him from view. She hoped he'd get the message and quickly hide.

The other girl gaped at her in surprise. "What are you doing?"

Marie continued to skip about and wave her arms. "Dancing. I'm trying to . . . um, keep warm," she fibbed hastily. "I came out here for some fresh air. But I forgot my coat, and it's a bit cold." She swirled around in a circle and saw with surprise that Starshine hadn't moved. He was watching her, his mouth twitching with amusement.

"That is a very good dance," he snuffled.

Marie did a double take. What was going on? How come Starshine had just spoken in front of Shannon? And why didn't she seem to see him?

The other girl's lip curled. "You can stop that stupid dancing. Do you think I don't know what you're up to? You were going to sneak home, weren't you?"

Feeling a little silly now, Marie came to a sudden halt. "What do you care? It's not as if anyone's going to miss me—especially you."

"I knew it!" Shannon crowed triumphantly. "Let's see what Mr. Carpenter has to say when I tell him!"

"Wait!" Marie called, but the other girl was already heading back toward the classrooms. "Oh, great," she groaned.

"Is something wrong, Marie?" Starshine snorted in concern.

Marie nodded. "I hate this school. I was just about to leave when you appeared. But it's too late now . . ." Starshine listened closely, his velvety nose twitching as she explained that no one seemed to want to be her friend.

"I suppose I'd better go back into class, or there'll be a huge mess," Marie sighed. "How come Shannon didn't notice you?"

"I used my magic. Only you can see and hear me," Starshine told her.

"You can make yourself invisible? Wow! You'll definitely be safe behind the bleachers then. So I'll see you after school?"

Starshine put his head on one side. "No, Marie. I will not be here."

Marie felt a stir of panic at the thought that he was going to leave. She'd hardly got used to the idea of having him as a friend.

"But where are you going?" she asked, worried. She knew it. The first real friend she'd made and he was leaving already!

Chapter THREE

The reindeer pawed the ground excitedly with one front hoof. "I am coming into school with you!" he exclaimed in a soft rumbling bellow.

"Really?" Marie felt a big grin spread across her face. This was awesome. She was finally going to have a friend in her class! But who'd have thought it would be a magic reindeer?

"How's that going to work?" she wondered aloud. "You're too big to hide under my desk or sit on my lap. Even if you're invisible, people could still bump into you and you could get hurt."

Starshine's dewy eyes twinkled mischievously.

Marie felt another warm prickling sensation at the back of her neck as the tiny golden snow globe began to glow brightly again. There was a flash of silver and gold starry light, and the reindeer disappeared. In his place stood a tiny stuffed version of himself.

"Wow! That's amazing," Marie said breathlessly, reaching down to pick up the toy.

Starshine just fit into her cupped hands. He had the tiniest, sweetest little

hooves, cute ears and antlers, and beautiful brown eyes. As she stroked his petal-soft white fur, she thought that she'd never felt anything so gorgeous and velvety. Starshine snorted with pleasure.

He was gorgeous as a young magic reindeer and magnificent as a glowing golden prince in his own icy world, but as a fluffy little toy, Starshine was totally adorable!

"Now you can come everywhere with me," Marie said enthusiastically. "You don't even have to worry about people seeing you. And you can sleep in my bedroom at home!"

"That sounds like fun. Thank you, Marie," Starshine said in a tiny voice that matched his new size.

As Marie went back into school, her heart felt lighter than it had in ages. Even the prospect of facing Shannon and Mr. Carpenter didn't seem that scary. With Starshine tucked inside her school sweater, she already felt braver and a little less lonely.

No one said anything as Marie came back into the classroom and made her way to her seat. She felt relieved. Shannon obviously hadn't carried out her threat about telling Mr. Carpenter that she was going to leave school in the middle of the day.

Marie glanced at the other girl as she passed her, about to say thanks for not tattling. But then she noticed her desk. It was a complete mess, with paints and paper and other art stuff all scattered around.

The glittery paper snowflake garland

she'd made earlier was in a crumpled pile on her chair. Marie went to pick it up, but it was stuck. Someone had obviously thought it would be funny to glue it to her seat.

Marie had a decent idea who that "someone" was.

Shannon had a knowing grin on her face. She looked as if she was trying hard not to burst out laughing. "Problem?" she asked Marie innocently.

Marie didn't answer. Sighing, she placed Starshine on the empty seat next to her and began clearing up the mess. The desk was soon back to normal, but her chair was a different matter. She could only tear off jagged bits of the paper snowflake. "I was really happy with that decoration. It's ruined now," she murmured sadly.

"Do not worry, Marie. I will help you!" Starshine said with an eager little snort.

Marie looked at him curiously. "But how? What if someone sees you moving?" she whispered.

"To everyone but you, I appear to be an ordinary stuffed toy."

"Oh, I get it. You're using your magic again! That's so cool . . ." Marie only just stopped herself from gasping aloud as she felt a familiar prickling sensation and the snow globe around Starshine's neck began glowing brightly.

Whoosh! A cloud of sparkling mist, made up of the tiniest gold and silver stars imaginable, swirled around her chair.

Crackle! The snowflake garland pulled

free, did a quick shimmy in midair, and draped itself across her desk.

"It's all in one piece again! That's amazing!" Marie exclaimed, and then hastily began to "cough" as Shannon looked at her in surprise.

Marie looked down at her desk, pretending to be busy in case the other girl started asking awkward questions. Shannon obviously couldn't see the cloud of magical mist drifting across the classroom.

"Whoa! Cool!" Chris suddenly burst out.

Marie turned around to see him holding two tubes of colored glitter that were spurting into the air like fireworks and showing no signs of stopping. Across the room, some cans of spray

snow made burping noises and squirted in all directions. Everywhere piles of decorations began to multiply, until the desks and floor disappeared beneath a thick layer of glittering snowflakes, paper lanterns, and paper chains.

Delighted kids leaped about, kicking up the snow and glitter, and throwing armfuls of decorations at each other.

"I think you used too much magic!" Marie whispered tactfully.

"But look how everyone is laughing and enjoying themselves! I have made everyone happy!" Starshine twirled his tiny tail, looking very pleased with his magical results.

"Mr. Carpenter isn't!" Marie warned. "Look!"

The teacher was wading through the fake snow, decorations, and heaps of red, blue, and silver glitter, which formed a knee-deep layer around him.

"Goodness me!" Mr. Carpenter gasped. "I'll have to tell the principal about this. We seem to have been sent some faulty art supplies."

"Do something, Starshine! Quick!" Marie hissed, seeing that things were quickly getting out of control.

The magic reindeer looked

disappointed, but his snow globe flashed again and the magical mist disappeared in a flash. The glitter, spray-snow fountains, and growing piles of decorations all instantly collapsed into shimmering dust and disappeared. Finally, the classroom was normal again.

"Phew!" Marie said, relieved.

Mr. Carpenter was scratching his head and looking puzzled. The teacher clapped his hands for silence. "All right, class. The fun's over. Settle down and get back to work, please."

"That was a lot of fun!" Chris said, appearing at Marie's side. He smiled broadly at her. "What happened?"

"Me? How should I know?" Marie said, shrugging as she bit back a grin.

Chris seemed friendlier all of a sudden.

She thought his smile looked genuine, but it was hard to tell.

"What are you asking *her* for? She doesn't know anything," Shannon said, sauntering over. She gave Marie a hard look and then gave Chris a dig in the side.

"All right. Keep your shirt on!" Chris said, but he grinned over his shoulder at

Marie as he moved away.

Shannon noticed and didn't look pleased.

What's she got against me anyway? Marie thought. To her surprise, she found that she wasn't quite as upset by the girl's meanness as usual. Having Starshine around made all the difference.

"My magic did not make everyone happy. Shannon was not very nice to you. I have done wrong. Perhaps I am not ready to be a proper White Crystal Reindeer," Starshine said, looking crestfallen.

"Yes, you are," Marie reassured him in a soft voice. "You meant well. You just went a bit overboard with your magic."

Starshine blinked at her. "What is 'overboard'?"

"It means . . . um, a bit too enthusiastic," Marie explained.

"I understand. I think that is what my father and older brothers would say, too," Starshine said sadly. His ears drooped and his chocolate-brown eyes lost a little of their twinkle.

Marie could see that he was missing his family. She made sure no one was looking, before drawing him into her lap. As she stroked him, her heart went out to her little friend.

"I know how you feel. I miss my dad like crazy. Maybe we can help each other not to feel so lonely?"

Starshine nodded and nuzzled her hand with his tiny velvet-soft muzzle.

Chapter FOUR

"Hi, Gran! I'm home!" Marie called as she entered the hallway after walking home from school.

Marie hung up her coat and took Starshine out of her schoolbag.

"This is a good place to stay until I find my way home," he said, looking around.

Gran appeared in the kitchen doorway. She spotted the magic reindeer before

Marie had a chance to smuggle him upstairs. "Hello, sweetie! What have you got there?" she asked.

"N-nothing!" Marie said in a panic, before she remembered that Gran could only see Starshine as a tiny toy reindeer. "I mean . . . um, one of the kids in class gave it to me."

"Well, that's nice," Gran said, smiling warmly. "It's a very cute toy. What dainty little antlers and hooves! I'm glad you're starting to make friends." She went to fill the kettle.

Marie followed her into the kitchen. She wondered what Gran would have said if she knew that her *only* friend was a magic reindeer. But, of course, she would never tell anyone Starshine's secret.

Then her mom arrived home from

work, and they all drank hot chocolate and ate cookies in the kitchen. Gran was saying how she wished they'd had a chance to decorate the house before Marie and her mom came to stay. "It's so scruffy-looking. It hasn't been done in a long time."

"It's fine, Mom. Don't worry about it," Mrs. Zaleski said.

Marie had Starshine on her lap, and she was carefully slipping him little bits of cookie. She noticed that he had pricked up his ears and was listening closely to Gran.

"The older lady is not happy with her house," the little reindeer snuffled thoughtfully.

"Mmm. A lot of grown-ups say stuff like that." Marie whispered, patting him. She was thinking about the cozy bed she would make for him in her room.

She tucked Starshine under her arm, drained her mug, and put it in the dishwasher. "I'm going to do my homework," she announced to Mom and Gran, before trudging upstairs. Marie's small bedroom overlooked the front yard and street. Beside the bed, there was just space for a wardrobe, a bookcase, and a chest of drawers. A dollhouse, which Gran had found at a tag sale, stood on top of the chest.

Starshine was on the bedside rug, watching as Marie fished around in the wardrobe for a shoe box.

"I thought you could sleep in this!" she said, folding up a wool scarf and putting it in the box. "And you can snuggle up with me at night."

Starshine immediately leaped into the box and lay down, folding his legs beneath him. He looked so cute that Marie couldn't help smiling.

"I like it here, but human houses are very warm," he panted, showing his little pink tongue.

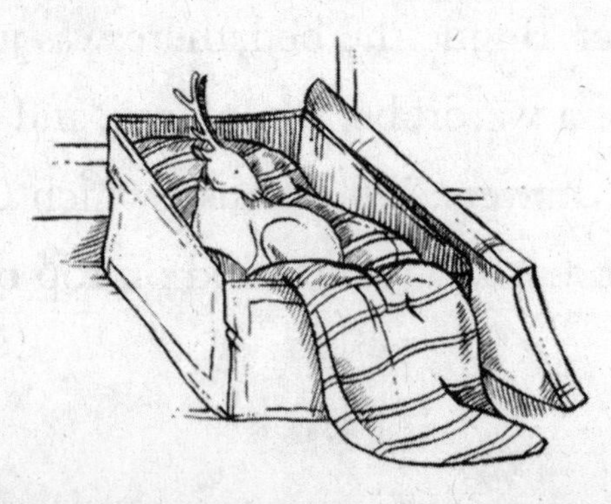

Marie remembered that her new friend came from a world of ice and snow and wasn't used to central heating in houses. "Oh, sorry! You must be absolutely boiling. I'll open my window."

She did so, and a blast of cold air filled the small room. Starshine lifted his head and his nose twitched with pleasure as he snuffed it up. "That is much better. Thank you, Marie."

"No problem," Marie said, hiding a shiver as she reached for another sweater. She didn't mind wearing extra clothes to keep warm, if it meant Starshine was comfortable.

She had a sudden thought. "You must be really hungry. Those pieces of cookie won't have filled you up. I can hear Mom and Gran in the living room. I'll sneak back downstairs to the kitchen and see what I can find. Back in a minute!"

Starshine's chocolate-brown eyes lit up. "That is good. My tummy is rumbling."

Luckily the kitchen was empty. Marie opened the fridge and looked inside, and then realized that she wasn't sure what reindeer ate. They were vegetarians, weren't they? On impulse, she grabbed a carrot and a couple of sticks of celery and then reached into the fruit bowl for an apple on her way out.

Back upstairs, Starshine eyed the fruit and vegetables warily. Reaching out, he sniffed the carrot and then took a tiny nibble. He nodded slowly, looking surprised, and then sampled the apple and celery. "Delicious!" he snorted, his eyes sparkling as he chomped. "I like human food."

"What do you usually eat?" Marie asked him.

"Grass, moss, and small plants we find by scratching away the snow," he told her.

Marie thought hard. She supposed he could eat the grass on the school playing fields, but Gran's yard didn't have a lawn. What was he going to eat at night and weekends? Mom or Gran were going to notice if she kept taking stuff from the fridge to feed him.

"I know! There's a pet store on the way to school. They've got a special offer on bags of hay. I can buy a small bag tomorrow and smuggle it home in my schoolbag."

"What is hay?"

"Dried grass, I think," Marie said. "It's what lots of animals eat, like . . . um, horses and rabbits."

Starshine nodded, licking his chops. "Hay sounds good."

Marie gently stroked his fluffy coat and warm little antlers. Starshine nudged her very softly and licked her fingers. His breath smelled warm and spicy like Christmas cookies. She felt a surge of affection for the tiny reindeer.

Just then she heard the phone ring downstairs in the hall.

"That might be Dad!" she said excitedly. "He usually calls around this time. Let's go and see!"

Starshine nodded his head.

Tucking him under her arm, Marie raced down the stairs two at a time and grabbed the phone.

"Hello, *aniołku*," said her dad's voice.

"Hi, Dad!" She loved the way he always called her his "angel." "How are you? How is Aunt Jolenta?"

Mr. Zaleski told Marie that her aunt was doing quite well, but he still couldn't leave her yet. They chatted for a few minutes. Marie told him about school and how things were a little better, but she didn't mention Starshine. He told her he missed her and then asked if she'd put her mom on the phone.

"*Kocham cię*, Marie."

"I love you, too, Dad," she said with a lump in her throat. "Please come here soon." Her mom had come into the hall and was standing beside her. Marie turned and passed her the phone.

As she wandered into the living room where Gran was collecting her library books and putting them in a bag, Marie blinked away tears. Now that she had Starshine for a friend, she didn't mind so much that she still hadn't made any friends at school. If only Dad could be here, then everything would be perfect.

"Do you two want to come to the library with me?" Gran asked when Marie's mom had finished talking to her dad.

Mrs. Zaleski nodded. "I could do with a change of scene. What about you, Marie?"

"I think I'll stay here," Marie decided, plunking herself on the sofa. She really wanted to curl up with Starshine and watch some TV.

But he had other ideas. As soon as the

car pulled out of the driveway, Starshine leaped off the sofa.

The moment his tiny hooves touched the carpet, he instantly grew to his normal size. "I know a way to make Gran happy with her house!"

Marie felt a warm prickling sensation at the back of her neck as Starshine's golden snow globe shone with power, and a sparkling gold and silver starry mist appeared.

Something very strange was about to happen.

Chapter FIVE

Marie watched in total astonishment as the magical starry mist swirled around the room.

Rumble! All the furniture disappeared and the walls stretched upward into jagged icy peaks and a white domed ceiling. *Crackle!* Ice sculptures, tables and sofas carved into the shapes of swans appeared. *Rustle!* Mountains of gold pillows plopped onto the sofas and a shining golden carpet unrolled across the floor.

"Oh!" Marie gasped, horrified.

"Do you like it? It is just like a room in Ice Mountain Castle," Starshine said proudly.

"It's . . . um . . ." She searched for the right word. "Different?" She didn't think this was what Gran had in mind.

Just then there was the sound of a car outside in the driveway. Marie rushed over to the window. "It's Gran and Mom! They must have forgotten something! Quick, Starshine, put everything back as it was!"

"But it is so beautiful. Are you sure?" he bleated, disappointed.

"Yes! We have to do it now!" Marie cried in a panic.

Time seemed to stand still. Once again Marie felt a prickling sensation as Starshine's snow globe instantly worked its magic. In a flash of bright gold and silver stars, everything in the room shrank in size and the golden carpet folded itself up around them. With a swishing sound it tightened like a drawstring. *Flash!* It disappeared, returning the icy room to normal.

Marie breathed a sigh of relief. It was only just in time. "Hi, Mom!" she said brightly, as Mrs. Zaleski peeked her head around the door.

"Hi, honey. Silly me! I forgot my purse—" Her mom broke off in surprise. "Wherever did that great big reindeer come from?"

"What reind—" Marie's eyes widened

as she realized that Starshine was still his full size and must have forgotten to be invisible. She whirled around to him. "Oh, *that* reindeer. It's . . . um, a prop for the class play," she improvised, giving Starshine a pleading look. Luckily, he caught on quickly and didn't blink or move a single muscle.

"It's much lighter to carry than it looks," Marie went on. "I said I'd . . . um, bring it home to . . . to spruce up the gold paint on its antlers. I'm taking it back with me tomorrow. I forgot to tell you."

Her mom nodded. "Good for you! It's great that you're starting to get more involved in school." She grabbed her bag from the table and went back out. "See you later!"

Marie waited until she heard the front door bang and the car drive away. "Phew! That was *too* close!"

Starshine hung his head and looked up at her with huge, sad brown eyes. "My magic went wrong again," he snorted regretfully. "And you could have been in terrible trouble. I am a very bad reindeer."

Marie's heart melted. She put her arms

around his neck and pressed her face to his fluffy warmth. "You're a good reindeer. The best there ever was and I love having you for my friend!" she said firmly. "You only want to make people happy."

Starshine pricked his ears and nodded. "That is true. The purpose of a White Crystal Reindeer is to deliver gifts and bring happiness."

"And that's a really kind thing to do. But you're not used to how things work here yet. So maybe you could check with me first next time, before you do any magic?" she suggested tactfully.

As she stepped back, she saw that Starshine's face was aglow and every trace of unhappiness had faded from his eyes. "You are so clever, Marie. That is exactly what I will do!" he promised.

"All right, class! We'll be choosing the lead parts for the school musical this morning! It's called *A Christmas Wish*," Mr. Carpenter announced the following day in the school hall.

"Yay! I've been waiting for this!" Shannon bounced up and down in her seat so that her shiny brown hair waved back and forth.

The teacher smiled as he took his seat at the piano. "Okay then, Shannon. Let's see what you can do."

Shannon sang a song from a well-known musical. She had a pleasant voice, but it wasn't very strong, and she wobbled on some of the higher notes. When she finished, everyone clapped. As Shannon went back to her seat, she smirked at Marie. "The part of Mary's got my name on it," she said confidently.

Marie sat quietly as various boys and girls came forward and sang the same song. Some were really good, but others were awful. It didn't matter. They all got a round of applause.

"Are you going to sing?" Starshine asked from where he lay in Marie's lap as a tiny, fluffy reindeer toy.

"I . . . I'm not sure I want to dare," Marie whispered to him. "Everyone here would only tease me."

In Poland, Marie had been in the choir at the local church. She loved acting and singing and would really have liked to be involved in the class play. But she didn't think it was worth making the effort. Anyway, the best parts were bound to be snapped up quickly.

"I think you should. I could help you get a part," the magic reindeer said eagerly, his tiny tail twirling.

Marie saw that the golden snow globe around his neck was beginning to glow.

"Remember what we said about doing magic?" she reminded him quickly. "It's not always the answer."

Starshine nodded, and the snow globe

returned to normal. Everyone had now returned to their seats. The teacher stood up and moved away from the piano. "Right, if there's no one else—" he began.

But Starshine's comment had made Marie think. She found herself putting him aside and getting to her feet. "I'd like to try for a part, please."

"Marie? Of course you can!" Mr. Carpenter smiled encouragingly as she walked toward him. He sat down at the piano and placed his hands on the keys. "Do you know this song?" He waited for her to nod. "All right then. Ready when you are."

Marie took a deep breath. Her hands trembled with nerves as she opened her mouth to begin. But only a dry croak came out.

Chapter SIX

Marie felt herself blushing as the whole class erupted with laughter.

"There's not a part for a frog in the musical!" Shannon jeered.

The teacher held up his hands for silence. "Marie's just nervous. Let's give her a chance." He turned back to Marie. "Take a deep breath. There's no hurry. You tell me when," he said, smiling encouragingly.

Marie fought the urge to sink back into her seat. Mr. Carpenter was being really nice. She swallowed hard as she forced herself to relax. "Ready."

As Marie began to sing, she felt her earlier nerves pouring away. Her pure, sweet voice rang out into the hall. She reached the final high note, holding it easily until the song ended and the teacher lifted his hands from the keys.

There was a moment of stunned silence. Marie's heart sank. She knew she shouldn't have stood up to sing in front of everyone. They must have hated it!

But then someone started clapping slowly. Someone else joined in and then another person and then another . . . Soon wild applause rang out. Everyone was clapping like mad, except for Shannon.

She just sat there with her mouth open. For once, she didn't seem to know what to say.

"Way to go, Marie!" Chris yelled. "That was fantastic!" Marie looked across at him. He seemed to really mean it. She gave him a shy smile of thanks and he grinned back happily.

"Oh, shut up, Chris! She wasn't that good!" Shannon snapped.

But no one else agreed with her. Students that Marie had hardly spoken a word to came over to congratulate her. They wanted to know if she'd had singing lessons or been to theater school.

Marie shook her head. "I just love singing," she explained, overwhelmed by all the attention.

"Well, I think we've found our Mary!" Mr. Carpenter said delightedly. "Marie Zaleski will be playing the lead part.

Marie waited until she'd changed out of her uniform after school before telling her mom the good news. She'd left Starshine munching hay in her bedroom.

"That's wonderful! My girl's going to be a big star!" Mom gave her a huge hug.

"Mo-om!" Marie said, grinning. "It's

only a teeny part in the class play!"

"Well, I'm very proud of you," her mom said. "Come on. We're going out."

"Where are we going?"

"To the new Polish deli on Main Street. I wanted to get some groceries anyway. We'll celebrate with something nice to eat."

"I'll just get my bag," Marie said happily. She scooted upstairs to ask Starshine if he wanted to come, too. He'd finished his hay and jumped readily into her bag when she opened it for him.

It was only a short drive to the new delicatessen. Marie stood looking in the window while her mom put coins in the parking meter.

"Wow! Isn't this place amazing?" she said to Starshine.

The tiny magic reindeer nodded. He had reared up and looped his front legs over the edge of her bag so he could see the jewel-colored jars of jams, fruits, and pickles. A rich smell of coffee and fresh bread floated through the open door.

"Hi, Marie!" called a cheerful voice.

It was Chris, walking toward her with a broad smile on his face.

"Oh . . . um, hi," Marie answered.

"Congratulations again for getting the part in the play," he said, pausing.

"Thanks," Marie said, surprised and pleased. She remembered how he had seemed friendlier toward her in class lately, despite Shannon's influence.

"This is a nice deli," Chris said, looking in the window admiringly. "But I can't tell what some of the stuff is, unless there's a picture on the label. I bet you know, though, right?" he said, flashing her one of his playful grins.

Marie nodded, feeling a little self-conscious. But after a moment's hesitation, she read some of the labels aloud.

Chris listened closely. "That's a really cool language," he said when she'd finished. "Could you teach me some Polish?"

"Maybe," Marie said warily, waiting for the usual silly comment. But it never came. She wondered if Chris was actually being serious.

Mrs. Zaleski was finished at the car. She came over to them. "This is Chris. We're in the same class," Marie told her mom.

"Hi, Mrs. Zaleski," Chris said politely.

"Hi, Chris. It's nice to meet one of Marie's new friends. Would you like to join us for some cake?"

Marie looked at the ground, horrified. She couldn't believe her mom had just done that! Of course Chris would say no.

"Yeah—sounds great! Thanks, Mrs. Zaleski. That's okay with you, isn't it Marie?" Chris asked.

"Yes, of course." Marie felt a shy smile starting to spread across her face. "I hope they've got some honey cake. You'll love it. And there's this amazing milkshake . . ."

Later that day, as she lay on her bed reading a book of animal stories, Marie was still thinking about what a good time they'd all had. Starshine was beside her.

"Can you believe it? Mom really liked Chris. She even asked him to drop by our house over Christmas vacation. And he said he would!"

Starshine yawned and stretched out his little legs. "I like Chris, too."

Marie nodded slowly. Chris was much nicer outside school. For the first time, she wondered if she might have found another friend.

Chapter SEVEN

Rehearsals for *A Christmas Wish* took place over the next week. Marie and the other kids playing lead roles worked hard at learning their lines and practicing their songs. "I'm going to be onstage almost all the time. I hope I can remember everything," Marie whispered to Starshine. She reached out and stroked his soft white fur as he stood on her desk in his toy disguise.

His big chocolate-brown eyes sparkled at her. "You will be very good. I am looking forward to the play."

Marie smiled fondly at her magical friend. "I'm a bit nervous, but I'm looking forward to it, too!"

Shannon appeared beside her desk. "I can't believe I lost the best part in the play to a kid who brings stuffed toys to

school!" she said with disgust. "And now she's *talking* to it! How pathetic is that!"

"There's nothing wrong with liking toys." Marie put her arms around Starshine protectively.

"Yeah—if you're about four years old!" Shannon's lip curled as she stood there with her hands on her hips.

Before Marie could think of a reply, Chris called out. "I've got a teddy bear my mom bought me when I was a baby. So I guess that makes me pathetic, too, doesn't it?" he said, flashing Marie one of his playful grins.

"That's, um, different. Everyone knows teddy bears are cool," Shannon said, flustered. "Anyway, why are you taking her side? I thought family was supposed to stick together. You're *my* cousin—in case you've forgotten."

"I know that, but Marie's new in class. There's no need to pick on her," Chris said.

"I'm not!" Shannon snapped back sulkily. "What about *her*? She thinks she's just so cool for stealing my part!"

"Just leave it, Shannon," Chris said, rolling his eyes. He got up and sauntered across the room to a piece of cardboard shaped like a manger, which he was helping to paint.

"Yeah! You're right. She's not worth it!" Sticking her nose in the air, Shannon flounced after him.

Marie sat in stunned silence. Shannon and Chris were cousins? She hadn't realized they were related because they had different last names.

"How stupid am I for even thinking that Chris wanted to be my friend?" she whispered to Starshine. "He was just pretending to be interested in learning Polish so he and Shannon could tease me even more!"

Starshine's little ears drooped. "I did not think Chris was a mean person."

Marie didn't either, but she wasn't sure any more. Feeling tears well up in her eyes, she blinked them angrily. *Who needs friends in class anyway*? she fumed silently. She already had the best friend anyone could ever have in her magic little reindeer.

Marie slipped out into the yard with Starshine that evening. White frost sparkled on a bush near the patio and their breath steamed in the cold air.

With an eager little snuffle, Starshine turned back to his normal size, although he remained invisible. He reached out to nibble a couple of leaves from the bush.

"It is very strange to live in a world without snow," he commented, chewing.

"It was snowing when Mom and I left Poland," Marie said. "I hope we get some here. A white Christmas would be wonderful."

"I should be delivering presents all over the world with the other White Crystal Reindeer," Starshine said wistfully. He looked up into the night sky, which was dotted with millions of stars. Suddenly he stiffened.

Marie followed his gaze. There, spreading toward the horizon, was a trail of faintly glowing silver and gold hoofprints.

"My herd! They have been here!" Starshine bleated excitedly.

She gasped. Did that mean that he would be leaving to go after them?

"Are . . . are you going to try to catch up with Moonfleet, Dazzler, and the others?" she asked anxiously.

The young reindeer shook his head. "No. The trail is cold and already fading.

But it proves they came this way. I will watch out for a fresh trail when they return. And then I may have to leave suddenly to follow them . . ."

"Oh." Marie felt a sharp pang as she thought of how lonely she would be without him. He was still her only friend. She realized that she would never be ready to lose him. "You . . . you could stay here with me if you wanted to," she said hopefully.

Starshine shook his head, his beautiful chocolate-brown eyes softening with affection. "That is not possible. I must return to my family in Ice Mountain Castle. I hope you understand, Marie."

Marie nodded sadly. She swallowed hard as she decided not to think about Starshine leaving. Instead, she promised herself that she was going to enjoy every single moment she had left with him.

Starshine bent his head and nuzzled her sleeve with his sensitive nose; a cloud of his warm sweet breath spread around her.

Marie put her arm around his neck and pressed her cheek to his fluffy warmth. "Let's go inside to my cozy bedroom and snuggle up together. It's freezing out here!" Starshine nodded, his golden antlers gleaming in the moonlight.

The next few days at school passed in a flurry of activity. Marie made sure she kept out of Shannon and Chris's way. But she caught Chris looking at her questioningly a few times. Once he started to come over to her, but she quickly walked away.

"I wish I could trust him," she confided to Starshine as they sat at her desk later. "But he's probably laughing about me behind my back with Shannon. They're always whispering together."

"I do not think Chris would do that," Starshine said. "Please do not be sad, Marie."

"Oh, I'm okay. I'm just a little annoyed, that's all," she admitted. "I'd started to like Chris."

"You need something to cheer you up!" Starshine decided, his eyes shining. "I have an idea! You were happy when you ate cake with your Mom and Chris in that store." His mouth curved as he showed his strong young teeth in an eager smile. Marie felt a familiar prickling at the back of her neck.

"Remember what we agreed about you being careful with your magic," she whispered warningly.

But it was too late. The snow globe around Starshine's neck began to glow and there was a bright flash, and a fountain of bright gold and silver sparks covered the empty chair beside Marie.

"Oh!" Marie blinked, rubbing her eyes as she noticed there was a big box full of delicious-looking cupcakes on the seat.

Starshine looked pleased with himself. "Now you can share these with everyone and have a good time!"

"Wow! These are gorgeous!" Marie felt relieved that, this time, Starshine didn't appear to have done anything too dramatic. She eyed the yummy cupcakes. They had frilly paper cases and pink, yellow, or white icing with glittery rainbow-colored sprinkles.

She picked up the box and took it over to the teacher. "I brought these for everyone to share. Would you like a cupcake, Mr. Roberts?"

The teacher's face lit up. "That's extremely kind of you, Marie. They look delicious." He took a bite. "Mmm, interesting flavor. Lemon and . . . is that sausage-flavor icing? Did you make them yourself?"

"Um . . . yes," Marie lied quickly,

hiding her surprise at the oddly flavored cupcake. She hurried across the classroom and offered the cupcakes to a group of kids who were painting scenery.

As kids helped themselves and began eating there was a ripple of excitement. "Cool! Mine's banana with ketchup-flavor icing!"

"Try this one! It's cucumber with chocolate!"

Marie smiled. As usual, Starshine had meant well, but in his enthusiasm he'd managed to mess up his magic! Luckily, everyone was having great fun sampling the weird flavors.

By the time Marie worked her way around to Chris and Shannon there were only three cupcakes left. Two ordinary-size ones, and a really large luscious one with extra rainbow sprinkles. Marie frowned. She was sure that the extra-big cupcake hadn't been there earlier.

Glancing across at Starshine, she noticed that he wore a mischievous expression. *What's he up to now?* she wondered.

"Thanks for bringing these in," Chris said, smiling at Marie. "I hope they're as

good as that honey cake we had the other day with your mom."

"What honey cake?" Shannon said suspiciously, shoving past him to take the larger cupcake.

Shannon gave Marie a triumphant look as she took a huge bite. Suddenly her eyes bulged and she turned a sickly color. Diving across the classroom, she picked up the trashcan and practically stuck her head into it. "Yuck!" she spluttered, spraying cupcake crumbs everywhere. "Cough medicine with sardine-flavor icing!"

Chris burst out laughing. "Shame! Mine's strawberry with orange icing! Serves you right for being greedy! Great cupcakes, Marie."

As Marie returned Chris's smile, she started to feel bad about avoiding him.

He obviously hadn't told Shannon about the Polish deli. Maybe he didn't want his cousin to make mean comments or tease Marie about it. Marie wondered if she'd misjudged him and whether they might still be friends after all.

Chapter EIGHT

"Why does my magic keep going wrong?" Starshine asked mournfully when Marie finished giggling about the unusual flavor combinations of yesterday's cupcakes.

It was Saturday morning, and the two of them were snuggled up under the comforter.

"Well, maybe you still need to think a

little bit more before you do something," she suggested, stroking his tiny soft ears. "Dad always tells me that." She felt a flicker of sadness at the thought of her dad and wished he could be here to watch her in the class play.

Starshine sighed, nodding. "My father always says this, too. It is hard to do this when I just want to make everyone happy."

"I know. I suppose it's something you'll get better at with practice," Marie said soothingly. "Anyway, it didn't matter about your magic going wrong in class. Everyone had the best time—except for Shannon," she remembered with a chuckle. "That extra-big cupcake was genius!"

Starshine still looked subdued. He

twisted his head around and began glumly grooming his fluffy fur.

"You need cheering up!" Marie decided. She leaped out of bed and quickly dressed. "Come on!"

"Where are we going?"

"To the shopping mall. There's a Christmas fair going on! Let's go and see if Mom will take us."

Her toy-size friend leaped up eagerly, his tiny tail twirling, and they went downstairs together.

"What a good idea," Mrs. Zaleski said, when Marie asked her. "Maybe Gran and Gramps would like to come, too." After breakfast, everyone piled into the car and headed for the mall. Her mom parked in the parking garage and then they all piled in to the elevator.

"Here we go!" Gramps pressed a shiny button that said SHOPPING.

The sound of Christmas carols filled the air as the elevator doors opened. Marie and Starshine walked toward an open area that was surrounded with stores. It had been transformed into a winter wonderland.

Silver icicles and waterfalls of lights hung from every surface. Dozens of silver stars covered the ceiling and there was a giant Christmas tree sprayed with fake snow and glimmering with decorations. There was a big Christmas market, too.

Starshine peered out from the safety of Marie's bag with eyes as big as saucers. "This is wonderful!" he said happily. "It reminds me of Ice Mountain Castle."

"I'm glad you like it," Marie said,

pleased that her idea to cheer him up appeared to be working. He seemed happier already.

Mom, Gran, and Gramps wandered around looking at the stalls that were piled with cakes, cookies, and all kinds of treats. There were wreaths, paper hats, and cans of silly string, as well as dozens of different decorations for sale.

Starshine's nose twitched at the smell of roasting chestnuts. Marie bought some and fed him tiny bits when no one was watching.

"Ho! Ho! Ho!"

With a jingle of sleigh bells, a white-bearded Santa in red robes trimmed with white fur appeared at the edge of the crowd. His gleaming sleigh was piled high with gifts and pulled by two real adult reindeer with spreading antlers.

Kids crowded close as Santa began giving out gifts, and Starshine spotted the two reindeer. He almost fell out of Marie's shoulder bag with excitement—his ears swiveled all over the place and his fluffy fur stood on end.

"Moonfleet! Dazzler! What are you doing here in disguise?" he brayed in delight.

Before Marie realized what was

happening, Starshine's snow globe glowed brightly and there was a flash of gold and silver sparks visible only to Marie as Starshine leaped high in the air. When they cleared, she saw that the magic reindeer stood there at his normal size.

A group of small children cheered and clapped. Luckily, everyone seemed to think that Starshine was part of the display.

"Wow! What a cute little white reindeer," one of them piped up.

"Look at his long lashes and pretty brown eyes," said a little girl.

As Starshine looked more closely at the two reindeer he seemed to realize his mistake. His head drooped. They were not his older brothers at all—they were just normal reindeer from this world.

Children were gathering excitedly

around Starshine. "Have you got presents for us, too?" a little boy asked.

Starshine turned around and around in circles. He looked confused by all the attention. But a pleased smile spread across his face as the crowd of kids pressed closer, patting him and stroking his soft white fur.

"Shall I use magic to make presents for them all?" he asked, looking uncertainly at Marie.

"No! Don't! It'll be total chaos!" she warned. Starshine was in danger of giving himself away at any moment.

Santa had noticed the commotion. "Oh! What's that white reindeer doing here?"

"Uh-oh!" Marie said under her breath, sensing trouble.

Santa walked toward Marie. His cheeks glowed an angry color that matched his red suit. "This is my spot. Have you got a license? Someone call security!" he shouted.

"Starshine! Make yourself tiny again," Marie whispered in a panic. "We need to get out of here . . . now!"

She felt a familiar prickling sensation at the back of her neck as the snow globe glowed again and Starshine seemed to disappear in the final flurry of gold and silver stars.

While Santa was still looking around for security, Marie bent down and swiftly picked up the toy reindeer before anyone stepped on him. Luckily, everyone else was looking at the shouting Santa and not at Starshine. She tucked him safely in her bag and began weaving through the crowd to where she could see her mom and grandparents.

"Oh there you are, sweetie," Mrs. Zaleski said. "Come on. We're about to have some hot chocolate and gingerbread."

"Great idea!" Marie said, breathless with relief.

She slipped one hand inside her bag and stroked Starshine, who rubbed his cheek against her hand and snuffled the tips of her fingers as a way of saying thank you.

A secret smile curved Marie's lips. Life was certainly never dull with Starshine around!

Chapter NINE

The morning of the class play dawned clear and cold. It was the day before Christmas Eve. The scenery was in place. The stage looked wonderful. Everything was ready.

Marie peeked out from behind the curtains at the packed school hall. She could see Mom, Gran, and Gramps in the audience. Her tummy cramped with nerves, and her fingers trembled as she smoothed her long blue costume and adjusted her headdress.

"Places everyone, please," Mr. Carpenter said.

Marie held her breath as the curtain began to rise.

Mr. Carpenter began playing the intro to the first song. Marie froze. Her tummy

and she felt sick. Could she really do this?

But she took a deep breath, stepped forward, and came in right on cue. Her voice wavered a bit, but she kept singing. Marie glanced into the wings. She saw Chris dressed as a shepherd in a tunic and a headdress made from a checked dish towel. Shannon stood next to him in an angel costume. Chris smiled and gave Marie a thumbs-up sign.

Then he nudged his cousin and—wonder of wonders—Shannon frowned, but did the same!

Marie smiled at them both gratefully. Her nerves had totally disappeared, and her voice swelled out strongly until it filled the hall with sweet, clear notes.

After that, the time seemed to fly. Everyone remembered their lines, and it all went well. Shannon sang her song and then passed Marie on the way to the wings.

On impulse Marie mouthed *good job* at her. Shannon blinked in surprise.

Suddenly the play was at an end. The audience clapped and cheered. Marie and the other players returned for not one but *three* curtain calls.

"They loved it!" Marie whispered delightedly to Starshine as she changed out of her costume.

Starshine beamed all over his face. His little golden antlers were glowing softly. "It was wonderful," he said breathlessly. "Everyone is so happy."

"You were pretty good," Shannon said at Marie's side.

"Thanks. So were you," Marie said.

"Look. Chris says you're okay, so maybe we should try to get along," Shannon murmured, staring at the ground. "I don't mean best friends or anything, though!"

Marie nodded, shocked into silence.

As the other girl walked away, she looked at Starshine in amazement. "Can you believe it? Shannon James just spoke to me nicely—for the first time! You didn't have anything to do with it, did you?" she asked suspiciously.

The magic reindeer shook his head. "Certainly not! I have learned my lesson. Now I think first before I do any magic!"

Marie felt a surge of pride for her friend. "That's fantastic. Good job, Starshine!" she praised. "The other White Crystal Reindeer will be proud of you."

Starshine's chocolate-brown eyes

glowed with happiness.

After she'd changed, Marie met Mom, Gran, and Gramps in the hall. They all walked home together. Marie saw Chris with his parents; she waved to him and he waved back. "See you tomorrow at your house," he called. "Your mom's invited us all."

"Great! Look forward to it!" Marie called back happily. She loved Christmas Eve. In Poland it was the main celebration—families got together to eat delicious food and open their presents. With her new friend joining them it was going to be extra special. She just wished her dad could be there, too.

She and Starshine were almost home now. Her mom and grandparents had just gone inside when the magic reindeer gave an excited little snort and looked up at the sky.

Marie did the same. She gasped as she saw the sight she'd been hoping for and dreading at the same time: a silvery line of shining reindeer hoofprints soaring overhead.

She froze. Starshine's White Crystal Herd was here. There was no mistake.

Starshine leaped out of Marie's bag with a flash of gold and silver light. He stood there as his real magical princely self: a young pure-white reindeer, with shining golden antlers and hooves. There was a halo of bright light all around him and gold dust gleamed in his fur.

"Starshine!" Marie gasped at his

regal beauty, blinking hard. She'd almost forgotten how marvelous he looked surrounded by that dazzling glow. "You're leaving right now, aren't you?" she asked, her voice breaking.

Starshine's chocolate-brown eyes lost a

little of their twinkle as he smiled sadly. "I must if I am to catch up with my father, Dazzler, Moonfleet, and the others."

A deep sadness washed over Marie, but she knew that Starshine had to leave and that she must be brave. She threw her arms around his shining neck. "I'll never forget you!"

Starshine allowed her to hug him one more time and then gently pulled away. "Farewell, Marie. I will not forget you, either," he said in a soft velvety voice. "Have a wonderful Christmas!"

The snow globe glowed brightly and a fountain of silver and gold sparkles sprinkled around Marie and tinkled as they hit the ground. Starshine leaped up into the sky; he faded and was gone.

Marie stood there with tears

pricking her eyes. She knew she would always remember the amazing adventure she and Starshine had shared. Something cold brushed her skin. It had begun to snow.

Marie looked up into the sky with delight. Snowflakes were falling thick and fast. She heard her mom calling her from inside the house. She was just about to go in when something made her look over her shoulder.

A familiar figure was walking toward her.

It couldn't be. Could it?

Marie blinked away the snowflakes on her eyelashes as a surge of pure happiness glowed through her.

"Dad! Oh, Dad! It's really you!"

Laughing and crying at the same time,

she flew toward him and threw herself into his arms. He gave her a big hug. "Hello, angel," he said in English.

He took a present wrapped in sparkly paper out of his pocket. "Open it now. This one's special."

Marie tore open the wrapping and looked at a tiny snow globe in wonder. Inside was a tiny white reindeer with lots of other reindeer around him.

"I'm glad you made it home safely, Starshine!" she whispered. "Thank you for being my friend."

About the AUTHOR

Sue Bentley's books for children often include animals, fairies, and wildlife. She lives in Northampton, England, and enjoys reading, going to the movies, and watching the birds on the feeders outside her window. She loves horses, which she thinks are all completely magical. One of her favorite books is *Black Beauty*, which she must have read at least ten times. At school she was always getting told off for daydreaming, but she now knows that she was storing up ideas for when she became a writer. Sue has met and owned many animals, but the wild creatures in her life hold a special place in her heart.

Don't miss these Magic Ponies books!

#1 A New Friend

#2 A Special Wish

#3 A Twinkle of Hooves

#4 Show-Jumping Dreams

#5 Winter Wonderland

#6 Riding Rescue

Don't miss these Magic Kitten books!

#1 A Summer Spell

#2 Classroom Chaos

#3 Star Dreams

#4 Double Trouble

#5 Moonlight Mischief

#6 A Circus Wish

#7 Sparkling Steps

#8 A Glittering Gallop

#9 Seaside Mystery

A Christmas Surprise

Purrfect Sticker
and Activity Book

Starry Sticker
and Activity Book

Don't miss these Magic Puppy books!

#1 A New Beginning

#2 Muddy Paws

#3 Cloud Capers

#4 Star of the Show

#5 Party Dreams

#6 A Forest Charm

#7 Twirling Tails

#8 School of Mischief

#9 Classroom Princess

#10 Friendship Forever

Snowy Wishes

Don't miss these Magic Bunny books!

#1 Chocolate Wishes

#2 Vacation Dreams

#3 A Splash of Magic